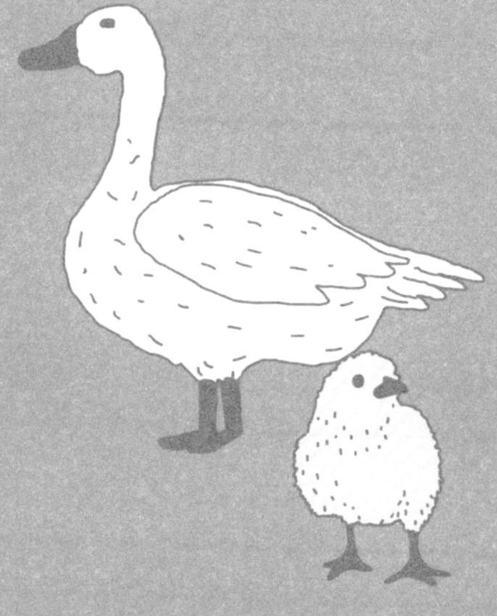

Property of:

____

F·R·I·E·N·D·S
The Television Series

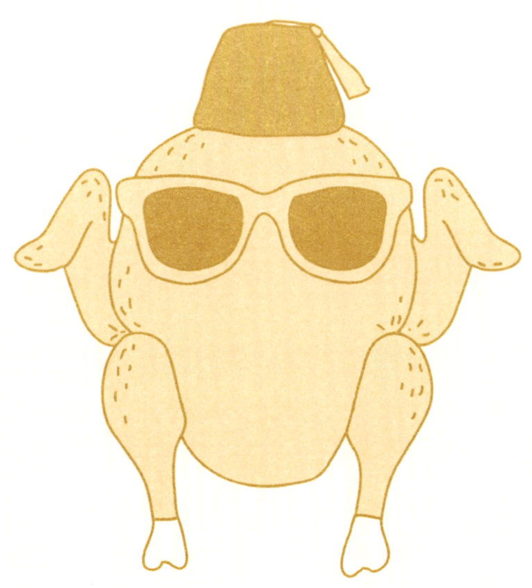

INSIGHTS
an imprint of
INSIGHT EDITIONS
www.insighteditions.com

MANUFACTURED IN CHINA

10 9 8 7 6 5 4 3

He's a Transponster

You're my Lobster

UGLY

HOW YOU DOING?

F·R·I·E·N·D·S

Your Little Harmonica

Miss Chanandler Bong!

PIVOT!

IT'S A MOO POINT

JOEY DOESN'T SHARE FOOD!

GUY

NAKED